Carl at the Dog Show

Carl at the Dog Show

ALEXANDRA DAY

Margaret Ferguson Books

Farrar Straus Giroux

New York

FOR ZUBIAGA,

whose bright spirit will never be forgotten
by those who knew him

"We're going to the dog show today
to watch Valerie and Carl's brother Gamble."

COUNTY ANIMAL SHELTER
Foster a Dog or Cat

 CHIHUAHUA

 CLUMBER SPANIEL

 DACHSHUND

 DALMATIAN

 ENGLISH COCKER SPANIEL

 GERMAN SHORTHAIRED POINTER

 GOLDEN RETRIEVER

 GREAT DANE

 GREYHOUND

 HUSKY

 IRISH SETTER

 IRISH TERRIER

 IRISH WOLFHOUND

 KOMONDOR

 MASTIFF

NEWFOUNDLAND

NORWICH TERRIER

OLD ENGLISH SHEEPDOG

PAPILLON

POMERANIAN

POODLE

PORTUGUESE WATER DOG

PUG

ROTTWEILER

SAINT BERNARD

SCOTTISH TERRIER

SMOOTH FOX TERRIER

TIBETAN TERRIER

WIRE FOX TERRIER

*Paste
your dog's
photo
here*

MY DOG

My thanks to the following people and animals who kindly assisted with this book: Nevia Faline Arnold and her parents, Valerie Vigesaa and Gamble (Ch. Wisteria's Las Vegas von Wilhelm), Christina and Sacheverell Darling, Matt Calkins and Cody, Cleo, Eamon, and Mr. Cat

Distributed in Canada by D&M Publishers, Inc.
Printed in China by South China Printing Co. Ltd.,
Dongguan City, Guangdong Province
First edition, 2012
1   3   5   7   9   10   8   6   4   2

mackids.com

Library of Congress Cataloging-in-Publication Data
Day, Alexandra.
    Carl at the dog show / Alexandra Day. — 1st ed.
        p.   cm.
    Summary: Carl the rottweiler explores the dog show in which his brother Gamble competes.
    ISBN: 978-0-374-31083-7
    [1. Dog shows—Fiction.   2. Rottweiler dog—Fiction.   3. Dogs—Fiction.]   I. Title.

PZ7.D32915Carh 2012
[E]—dc22
                                                                                                            2010044121

The Carl character originally appeared in *Good Dog, Carl* by Alexandra Day,
published by Green Tiger Press